P9-EDY-274

My New Kitten

JOANNA COLE

Photographs by MARGARET MILLER

MORROW JUNIOR BOOKS NEW YORK

I am extraordinarily grateful to Bonnie Ben Pilar for graciously allowing me to photograph her Maine Coon cat, Goddess, and Goddess's litter of kittens. I also want to thank Samantha Segan, a little girl who adores animals and has a wondrous way with cats. Bonnie, Samantha, and Goddess and her kittens made this project a pleasure.

The text type is 16-point Dutch 823.

Inquiries should be addressed to William Morrow and Company, Inc.,
1350 Avenue of the Americas, New York, NY 10019.
Printed in Singapore at Tien Wah Press.
1 2 3 4 5 6 7 8 9 10

Library of Congress Cataloging-in-Publication Data
Cole, Joanna. My new kitten/Joanna Cole; photographs by Margaret Miller. p. cm.
ISBN 0-688-12901-3 (trade)—ISBN 0-688-12902-1 (library)
1. Kittens—Juvenile literature. [1. Cats.] I. Miller, Margaret, ill. II. Title.
SF445.7.C645 1995 636.8'07—dc20 94-20295 CIP AC

To Katy, my first cat
—J.C.

For Kanooka
—M.M.

Whenever I go to Aunt Bonnie's house, I see her cat, Cleo.
I love Cleo, and she loves me.

One day, I noticed that Cleo looked fatter than usual. Aunt Bonnie said it was because she was going to have babies.

There was a whole litter of beautiful kittens inside her.
I couldn't wait to see them!

Soon, Cleo had her kittens.
She pushed each one out of her body.

The newborn kittens looked wet and bedraggled at first.
But Cleo washed them off with her warm pink tongue.

There were five kittens altogether. Cleo helped each one find a nipple. Then she curled up around them and let them nurse. I could hear her purring like crazy.

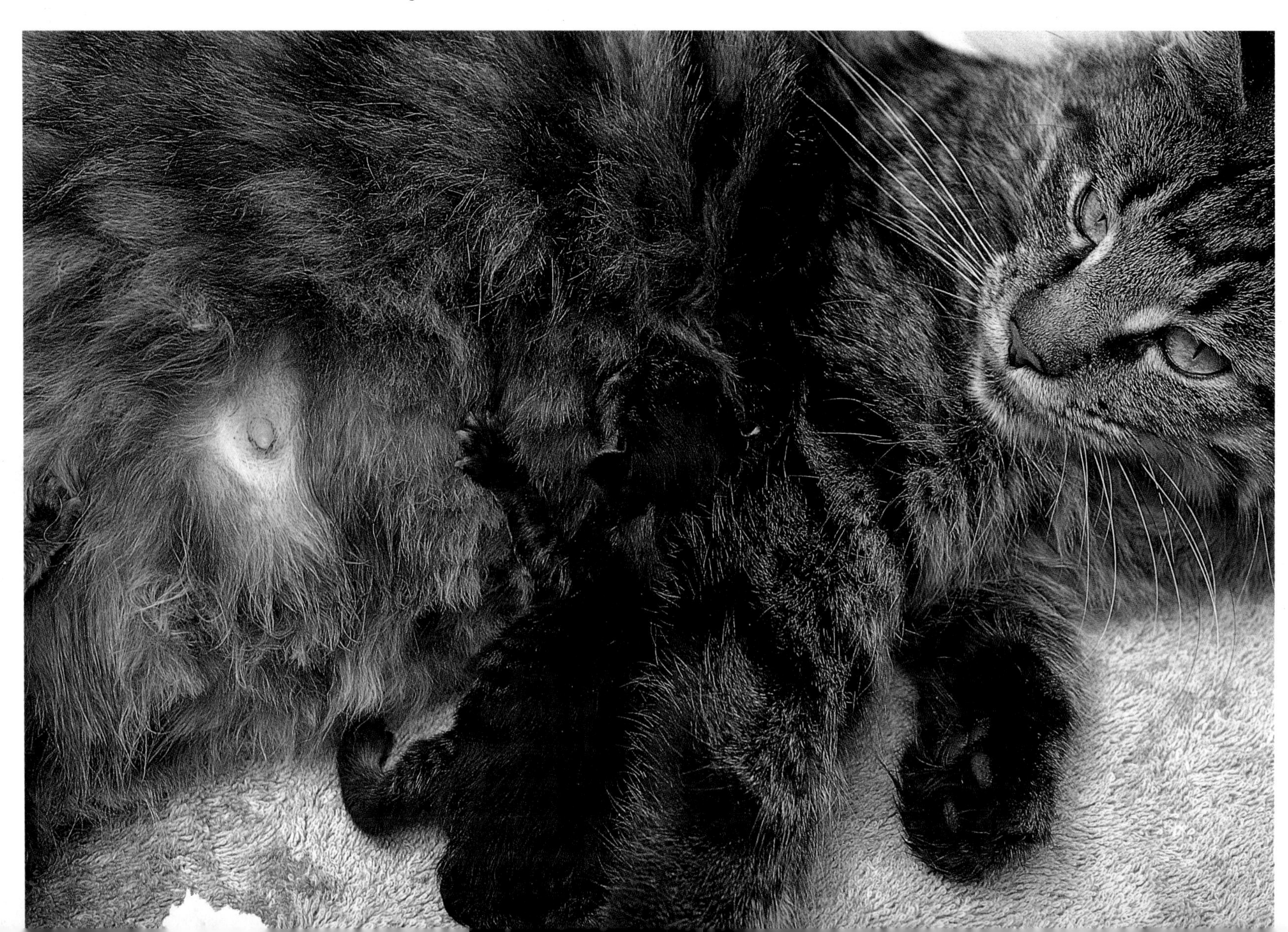

The kittens were so cute, I didn't want to leave them.
But it was time for me to go home. Aunt Bonnie said
I would see a big change the next time I came.

She was right! The next week, the kittens were bigger and furrier and cuter. And guess what! Aunt Bonnie said I could have one for my own.

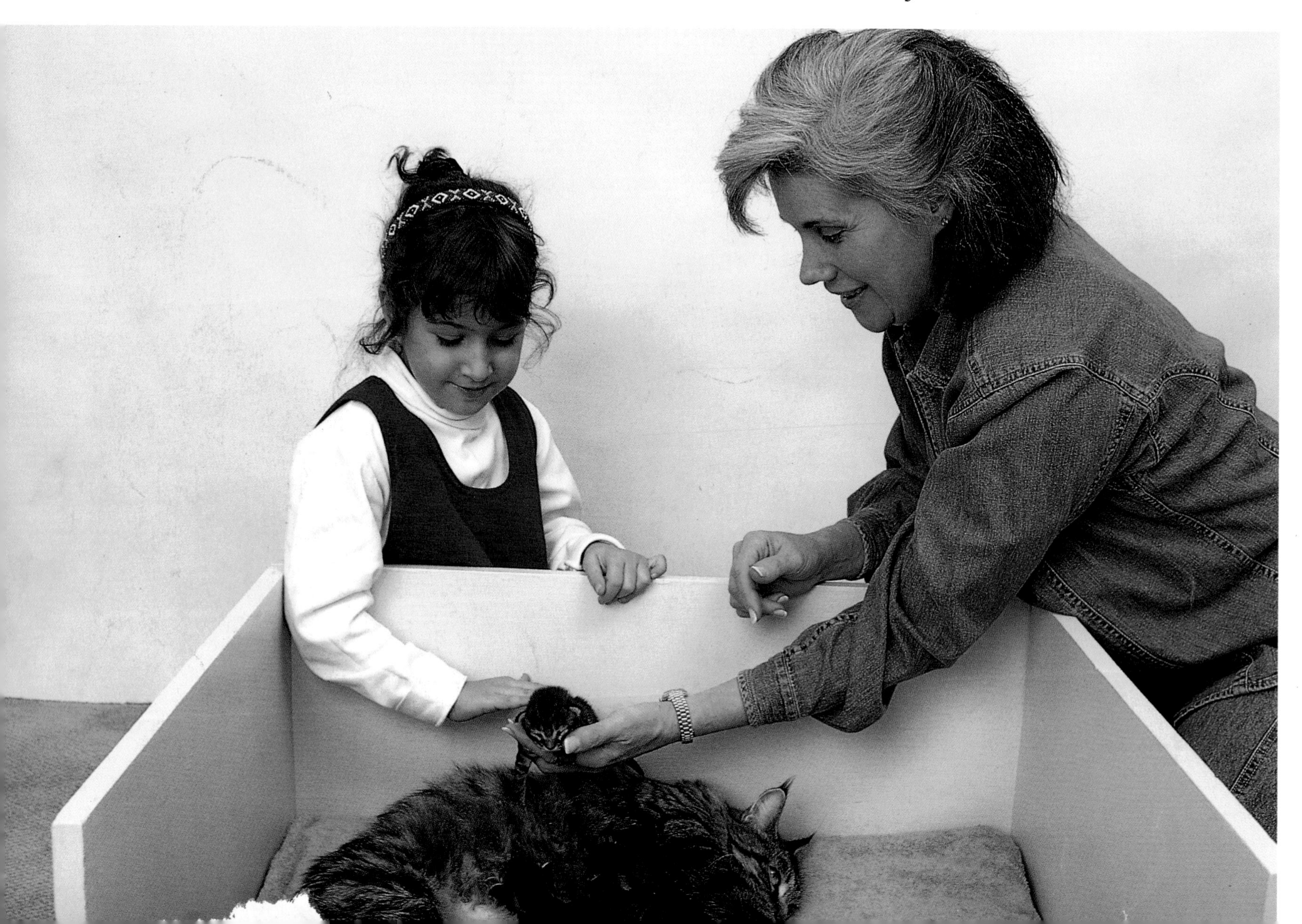

I picked this kitten. He was the first one to open his eyes.
I named him Dusty because he's gray.

Dusty was still too little to come home with me. When he was away from his mother, he started to cry.

He tried to find her, but he couldn't walk yet.

Cleo heard him mewing and came to get him.

She picked him up gently by the loose skin on his neck
and carried him back to the box.

Cleo wanted the kittens to stay close to her. They still needed their mother to wash them and feed them . . .

and to keep them warm as they slept.

It was fun to watch the kittens grow. The next time I saw them, they were three weeks old.

Dusty could almost stand up now.
And he could crawl pretty well.

The kittens were still getting milk from Cleo. But they were so big there wasn't room for all of them at the same time!

Now Cleo could leave them alone for a while. When she went away, they cuddled up to stay warm.

In another week, the kittens were even more grown-up.

For the first time, they were washing themselves.

And they had started play-fighting. They looked fierce, but they didn't really hurt each other.

By now, Dusty was getting curious about what was *outside* the box.

When I came the next week, Dusty was trying out the kitty gym.
It wasn't easy to get up there . . .

but it was worth it!

Kittens learn a lot of new things by watching their mother.
They watched Cleo eating cat food. Then they tried it too.

They learned to use the litter box the same way.

Kittens also learn by playing and being curious.
What is a ball for? It's for Dusty to bat around with his paw!

What about a toy carrot? It's to chew on and wrestle with!

And a slipper is
for digging in.
If it's fun for one kitten,
it's more fun for two.

Here comes Dusty!

At six weeks old, Dusty liked to be hugged.

He liked to play with me.

And he loved to have his belly rubbed.

When Dusty was eight weeks old, Aunt Bonnie said
he was old enough to come home with me.

Now Dusty belongs to me. I play with him. I take good care of him. I love Dusty, and he loves me.